# Dragonfall 5
# and the Space Cowboys

## BRIAN EARNSHAW

The vintage star ship, *Dragonfall 5*, has broken
down in space again – there is nothing surprising
about that; Old Elias gets on with the welding,
while Big Mother calmly picks up her knitting.
But the ship has stopped right beside the
Broken World – and that's full of surprises!
Tim and Sanchez land right in the middle of a
space-ranchers' feud and a treasure hunt that
leads to many strange places and people and
the excitement is fast and furious.

BRIAN EARNSHAW

# Dragonfall 5
# and the Space Cowboys

*Illustrated by Simon Stern*

A Magnet Book

Other books *by Brian Earnshaw in Magnet Books*

DRAGONFALL 5 AND THE ROYAL BEAST
DRAGONFALL 5 AND THE EMPTY PLANET
DRAGONFALL 5 AND THE HIJACKERS

*These titles are also published in hardback*

First published in Great Britain 1972
by Methuen Children's Books Ltd
11 New Fetter Lane, London EC4P 4EE
Methuen paperback edition first published 1975
Magnet edition reprinted 1979
Text copyright © 1972 Brian Earnshaw
Illustrations copyright © 1972
Methuen Children's Books Ltd
Cover artwork copyright © 1979
Methuen Children's Books Ltd
Printed in Great Britain by
Cox & Wyman Ltd, London, Reading and Fakenham

ISBN 0 416 84250 X (paperback)

# Contents

1· Cowshed Six                    *page* 7

2· Ma Maxwell strikes                  36

3· Condavee Country                    52

4· Scientists are useful               73

5· Real neighbourly                    85

# 1 · Cowshed Six

*Dragonfall 5* had broken down in the middle of space. It had happened before and Big Mother said that it would probably happen again, so long as Old Elias did his own engine repairs. You cannot go about in a riveted vintage starship with separate star-drive and rocket engines, taking cargo from planet to planet, and expect to get everywhere on time. So Big Mother got on with her knitting, cooked rather better meals than usual, and watched the others tinkering about with the broken star-drive.

Usually, when something went wrong with the starship's sixty-year-old main engines, they managed to coast along on their rocket power to some sheltering planet. There they could make their repairs in comfort with good air to breathe and interesting new people to meet.

But this time, though they had managed to

find a good bright sun, it did not seem to have any planets spinning round it, only a few asteroids, which are just chunks of rock. So they parked in mid-space, with no night or day, and the sun shining all the time out of a sky that was almost black. There the old starship lay suspended, blue, silver and shining, with her short back-swept wings and her cobra-shaped head.

Old Elias got out his welding outfit to work with inside, and Tim and Sanchez put on their

space suits, their magnetic boots and their safety lines to do what he told them outside the starship.

At first it was very thrilling to hang out there with millions of miles of dark blue nothing behind you and your mother sitting quietly knitting a few feet away through the glass portholes, but the sun was very hot and Sanchez was hopeless at welding metal or, indeed, at anything mechanical. So he just had to hang on to his safety line holding things for Tim, who enjoyed machinery. The helmets got stuffy and the space suits collected moisture just like plastic macs.

It wasn't as if they were even getting very far.

After two work-times and two sleep-times Old Elias had to admit, 'Darned if we can get much further without a flask of mercury and a five by two strip of super-stressed tungsten!'

Since neither of these things were likely to come floating by in mid-space this was rather depressing. They all played spillikins for an hour, but some sort of space current had got up and *Dragonfall 5* was rocking so much that the spillikins kept falling down. So they had supper, climbed into their hammocks gloomily, and went to sleep in spite of the sunshine nagging through the portholes.

Sanchez woke up first from a dream with a lot of scratchy bumping noises in it. Thinking he must have imagined these noises he lay in his hammock wondering how soon it would be before they had to use their laser radio to call for help. It would cost a lot of money, and they were not very rich because *Dragonfall 5* was so small she could not carry much cargo.

'Murrrr!' a deep bellowing sound came from just above his head and a clanking,

scratching, banging on the walls of the starship.
'Murrrr!' it came again.

Jerk, their Flying Hound Dog, was leaping at the cabin door and everyone was awake now, but Sanchez was the first to a porthole to pull a curtain.

'Golly,' he said, 'it's a herd of cows!'

Alongside *Dragonfall 5* was a most unexpected sight. As far as they could see was a rippling field of blue grass that showed silver on its underside leaves. It was moving gently up and down like waves that never broke. Dotted all over the moving field was a herd of fifty or more cattle.

Most of them were busy eating but one of them, a young bull, was right up by *Dragonfall 5* and had got his front legs on the starship's short swept-back wing. He looked more puzzled than cross, and it was he who was making the bellowing sound.

All the cattle were black and white, smaller than ordinary cattle, more like Jersey cows in build but wilder looking.

'Will someone get that dirty critter off my clean wing!' said Big Mother. She had spent hours polishing with metal wool before they took off last time – she was very house-proud.

'But there's no air out there. How can they breathe?' asked Tim.

'What's on the other side?' asked Sanchez.

They all hurried across the cabin and looked out. There was nothing but the emptiness of space, the dark sky and the bright sun. *Dragonfall 5* was resting against the very edge of the floating field.

'Did anyone test for air with the spectroscope when we first stopped here?' asked Tim who was always practical. And of course no one had, but you don't expect air where there are no planets.

Tim went up to the controls and took the spectroscope out of its drawer. He whistled.

'A bit low in oxygen,' he said, 'but perfectly good air! Where in space has it come from?'

'Murrrr!' came again from outside and a dreadful scraping, as if the bull was rubbing his horns along *Dragonfall*'s side.

'Do you hear that!' exclaimed Big Mother, 'and you all stand there doing nothing!'

And before anyone could stop her, not that anyone would ever have tried, she had pressed the switches to the double doors, seized a broom from the corner, and rushed out to stop her precious paint from being scratched.

'Oops! Good grieving garden-stuff!' they

heard from outside. A thin, pure air filled the cabin, like that on top of a mountain.

'Quick,' said Sanchez, 'something's happened to her!'

'It'll be the bull that's in trouble,' said Old Elias, 'not your mother!'

Certainly, when they got to the cabin door, the bull was trotting awkwardly away, tossing his head and snorting, but Big Mother was in a worse state. She was hanging in mid-air,

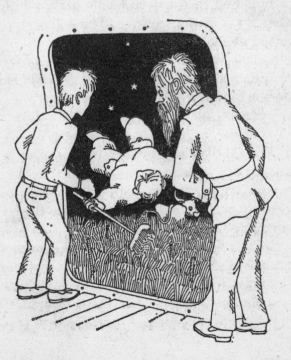

upside down, kicking and still holding the broom.

'There's no gravity to keep her down,' said Tim. 'Air but no gravity.'

'Boy!' said Big Mother severely, 'if you'll keep your science lectures to yourself and take hold of my broom handle I'll be grateful to you!'

Hurriedly they pulled their mother down to the gangway steps and set her right way up, puffing a little. She glared in the direction of the bull, and then moved firmly back into the cabin to her favourite couch. Tim and Sanchez winked at each other.

'Bull seems to be able to get along,' remarked Old Elias, staring out over the blue grass field. 'Do you see what big, flat hooves it's got?'

'Surface tension,' said Tim knowingly.

'What's that?' asked Sanchez.

'When there's no gravity, surfaces of things tend to stick to each other,' explained Tim. 'If we go out in our carpet slippers, carefully, we'll probably be able to get along. You see the bull isn't going very fast.'

'Do you notice those poles?' said Sanchez. 'They're planted all over the field. I bet they are to swing along on or hold on to. And there's some sort of building over there. Behind the ripples of grass, if you look carefully.'

He was right; so was Tim about surface tension. When the two boys got nervously down the gangway steps they found, first that the grass was quite firm and crisp, and second that if you balanced against the ripples that ran always under the surface you could stay upright and walk slowly forwards.

Sanchez took off once into the air because he pushed too hard with his feet, but Tim caught him by his belt and brought him down again. The brisk wind, the moving grass waves, the sun, and the snorting cattle were wonderful after being cooped up in *Dragonfall 5* for two weeks. Jerk loved it, too, but from time to time he had to be rescued after jumping into the air.

'We'll get a terrific sun tan at this rate,' said Sanchez, pulling off his shirt and slinging it over his shoulder.

'I'm a bit nervous of all these bulls,' said Tim. 'There are at least ten of them, and just because they ran away from Big Mother doesn't mean they'll run away from us.'

'I'd run away from Big Mother if I saw her walk out into thin air upside down,' giggled Sanchez. 'But you're right, and Jerk will be no use at all if they charge.'

They picked their way carefully to the building Sanchez had spotted. It was long and

low and rather battered, made of fibreboard.
Over the open end was written in faded letters:

## COWSHED SIX

Sanchez walked in. There was a strong smell
of straw and manure. A few chains hung from
the roof beams. What was that clumpety noise?

'Look out, Sanchez, he's charging!' Tim
called.

Too late to be of much use, Tim had seen
one of the bulls clumpetting over the grass
quite smartly in an odd shuffling run in which
none of its legs rose very high. Even so it had
almost lost control of where it went. Tim
dodged easily aside as it shook its horns at him,
snorted and plunged into the shadows of the
cowshed.

'Poor Sanchez,' he breathed. Jerk stood
behind him with his tail down.

From inside the shed came a great crashing
and snapping, a 'Hey!' from Sanchez and a
'Murrrr!' from the bull. Tim's worried face
peered round the corner.

Swinging from one of the beams was
Sanchez, still looking startled. The wall at the
far end of the shed, two walls in fact, had been
knocked clean out and the sunlight poured in.

The bull was bothered but unhurt about twenty yards beyond.

'He went clean through the wall!' said Sanchez. 'Pull me down, please. It's easier to get up than down with this gravity.'

Tim pulled him down, by his heel this time, and they went to see the ruin the charging bull had made.

He had gone clean through the fibreboard walls of a little room at the end of the shed. The only things that had been in it were a few empty bottles of cattle medicines and, lying plainly on the splintered boards, the shining length of a recording cylinder with a play-back button at the end. Sanchez picked it up.

'Odd thing to find here,' he said. 'I wonder what's on it?'

'There's an easy way to find out,' said Tim rather sharply. He reached over and twisted the play-back button. For a few moments the cylinder turned in silence. Then a clear, mocking voice began to speak.

'Well, nephews,' it said, 'so you found it after all! The code was a simple one but, with the education your parents gave you, I thought it would be too much for you. I knew that once you found the place you would tear it to bits. Such crudity.'

The voice on the cylinder laughed irritatingly and went on. 'Well, one hurdle is jumped, and two more to come. May I remind you to leave this recording cylinder here for my other dear nephews who are following you. It would not do to cheat, would it?'

Again the voice laughed. 'Now, no mystery to my second clue, only danger! The danger of new experience! You will find my second cylinder behind the most beautiful carving in the great cave of the Condavees. Good taste, my dear nephews, is everything, and remember,' (here the recorded voice became slow and serious), 'nothing, nothing, including the Condavees, is quite as you think it is. Goodbye dear nephews, as always, your affectionate Uncle Richard.'

The cylinder clicked to a standstill. Thoughtfully Sanchez wound it back again.

'What do you think of that, Tim?'

'We weren't really meant to hear it, were we? It's not our business, but it is very interesting.'

'Who is Uncle Richard, I wonder?'

'He sounded pretty superior and annoying,' said Tim, looking at the broken walls. 'I suppose the cylinder was hidden up there. We can't very well put it back again.'

'We'll ask Old Elias about it,' said Sanchez,

and put the mysterious cylinder in his pocket. 'Now let's see if we can move a bit faster by swinging from post to post.'

The only person who did not enjoy the next few minutes was Jerk who naturally could not swing from anything. If you zoomed round a post on one hand and threw yourself forward you could fly with your feet just scraping the grass for a clear twenty feet. Even if you missed the next post you fell downwards not upwards. The two brothers were soon expert, but you needed strong arms.

'This must be how you escape charging bulls,' said Tim. 'I like this place. I've never felt so free anywhere. Why isn't grass always blue? It's a much better colour than green!'

'Was that Old Elias calling?' asked Sanchez, cocking his head.

'No,' said Tim, 'Dad's back working on the star-drive. But I can hear it too, a kind of yodelling. It's up in the sky!'

Somewhere from the blue-black heavens a cheerful whooping and yippeeing was coming.

'There!' exclaimed Sanchez. 'Two people close together and one other behind them. Whatever are they riding on?'

'Can't be anti-gravs,' said Tim, 'because there's no gravity for them to work against.'

Down the shouting figures came. They swooped in a circle about twenty feet above *Dragonfall 5*, and then above the boys.

'Yuheeeeee!' called the foremost space rider, who waved an arm cheerfully to the boys and then swept on with his companions towards the cattle.

'They've each got dogs!' said Sanchez.

'Sitting on little saddles in front,' said Tim.

The riders were no older than the two boys but they had very brown faces, and wore tight fawn-coloured clothes. The things they were riding looked like enormous dumb-bells: a long shaft with a saddle in the middle and a big round silver ball at each end.

'They've dropped the dogs,' said Sanchez. 'They're rounding up the cattle!'

Swooping and diving, whistling their dogs and whooping loudly, the three riders were driving the snorting, lowing cattle together.

The boys had swung back to *Dragonfall 5*, and there they all watched fascinated as one of the riders drew a rope around three sides of a square, using the poles in the ground to hitch the rope to. Then, with a burst of barking, the three fuzzy brown dogs drove the cattle into the square, and the riders took the rope round the fourth side to pen them in. It was all

over in five minutes, and it left the floating field heaving gently like a ship after a storm.

This done, two of the riders got off their dumb-bells and swung quickly up to *Dragonfall 5* where they swept off their crash helmets politely and grinned at Big Mother.

'How d'ye do, ma'am!' said the taller of the two. 'It's good to see strangers. Welcome all to the Kench ranch! I'm Baz Kench and this here is my brother Alec. If you're havin' engine trouble we'd be proud to help you.'

Now that their crash helmets were off you could see they both had long black hair almost to their shoulders, and very white teeth. They were almost exactly Tim and Sanchez's age.

'That's very kind,' said Big Mother, getting up from her knitting chair and introducing everyone. 'And who is the third gentleman back there?'

'Oh that!' said Baz Kench with a surprised look, 'that's just our hired hand, Sparrer. Make your salute to the lady, Sparrer.'

Sparrer, who looked as if he wished Big Mother had not noticed him, nodded awkwardly and grinned, but he did not come forward. Sanchez was very impressed by the huge leather boots they all wore, and the heavy stunners they carried in their belts.

'You gentlemen don't happen to have a flask of mercury and a five by two strip of super-stressed tungsten back in your ranch, do you?' Old Elias asked very seriously.

'Why sir, I wouldn't know as to that,' replied Baz Kench, 'we not having had much of an education in what you'd call technology. But Great-Grandad saved a whole lot of bits and pieces after the Big Blow-up, and you're welcome to come and take a look at what we have.'

'We're on our way back now,' said Alec Kench, waving skywards with a big sweep of his arm. 'Should be home tomorrow, and if your two boys don't mind riding rough on the dog saddles we'd be glad to take them.'

'That's very kind,' said Big Mother, 'and I know the boys will be glad to go. But where is "home" exactly, and what place is this?'

'You mean you don't know where you've landed up?' asked Baz with a surprised look on his lean brown face.

'We know where we are going,' said Tim apologetically, 'but we often don't know quite where we are on the way!'

'Why this is the Broken World,' said Baz. 'You must have heard of it. Just a few chunks of rock spread over a few thousand miles, and the Kench ranch is on one of 'em. It's a fine homestead, though I say it as shouldn't. We run thirty thousand head of cattle on one cow pasture or another.'

'But what's broken?' asked Tim.

'Back in Great-Grandad's time there was a whole little planet here,' Baz explained. 'Not a great shakes of a place but good for cattle. Comes along what we call the Great War, and we got mixed up in it, don't know how. Some outsiders dropped what Great-Grandad calls a hydrogen fusion bomb into a deep bit of the sea. The whole lot breaks up. Zowey!'

'Didn't everyone get killed?' asked Big Mother.

'Most did. Some didn't. Great-Grandad said there was a real bad time for two, three years. Not much air. Spent all your time trying to breathe. Then something happened to some seaweed that got floating about in the air. I don't quite recall the word.'

'It mutated,' suggested Tim, 'changed into something else.'

'It's plain to see you've had some real education,' said Baz gravely, 'and we'll be more than proud to have you home with us. That's the word! This seaweed mutated into this blue grass pasture like you see here. It grew and it grew, and as it grew the air got better, and them as could went back to the cattle business again. And that's the Broken World.'

'What was it called before it broke?' asked Sanchez.

'Ain't no one remembers,' said Baz, 'or if anyone does they don't want to say. That's all over.'

'And there's only these little bits of rock and the blue grass?' asked Tim.

'There is one whole big piece way over yonder,' Baz waved behind them, 'but that's Condavee Country, bad land where poor white trash live. There's no one decent would go there.' He shook his head seriously.

Big Mother frowned a little at this but said nothing about it. Instead, 'Are those clothes of yours wired for heating,' she asked.

'Surely, ma'am,' replied Baz Kench politely. 'Our punch-riders'll do a hundred and up, and at that pace you're glad of hot pants and a warm backside, if you'll excuse me, ma'am!'

'Tim and Sanchez,' said Big Mother firmly, 'you'll wear your space suits except for the helmets, and no argument about it. And since these gentlemen have kindly offered to take you the less time you keep them waiting the better!'

'It's good to see someone as knows her own mind, ma'am,' said Baz, as seriously as ever.

'So perhaps you'll have a cup of tea with us while they're changing,' said Big Mother, determined not to be outdone in politeness by those newcomers.

'Whatever tea is, ma'am, we'll be glad to take it!' said Alec. 'Sparrer, hitch your punch-rider to the pasture and make ready for off. Before you leave give that steer a wash of rinsing fluid. I reckon it's coming on for a dose of brolick.'

So, while Sanchez and Tim got into their warm but clumsy space suits, Baz Kench and Alec Kench took tea with Big Mother. They did not think much of tea, but they were far too polite to show it. They told Big Mother that this particular floating field had been cut away from their Main Pasture two nights ago and they had been hunting for it until now.

'You mean a wind storm blew it loose?' asked Big Mother.

Baz and Alec scowled and their faces went dark.

'No ma'am, it was cut,' said Baz fiercely, 'cut by those thieving Maxwells! Might have been Ma Maxwell herself, she's still capable, but one of her gang for certain. Trying to steal fifty head of our cattle.'

'And it won't be long,' said Alec grimly, 'before we cut loose a hundred head of their cattle in return. Ain't no one going to tread around on the Kench ranch.'

'No sir!' agreed Baz.

Big Mother was beginning to wonder if this Broken World was a very safe place to let Tim and Sanchez go riding around in. But it was too late now to change her mind so, after making sure Tim had his miniature two-way radio to call for help if they really needed it, she let them go.

The four boys swung across to the punch-riders in a series of breathtaking swoops. Sparrer was keeping all three dogs. He was going to pull the field slowly back through the air to the main Kench pasture lands, while the rest rode ahead.

The punch-riders were quite old and shiny with use when you looked at them closely. There was nothing to hold on to with your hands, and Sanchez was worried he might fall off and shame them.

The Kench boys explained that the foot stirrups guided the punch-riders: right foot down – move up, left foot down – move down, and you steered by swinging your body.

Tim and Sanchez took their seats on the little dog saddles very uneasily: it would never do to ask for something to hold on to. They waved back to *Dragonfall 5*.

'So long, Sparrer!' called Alec.

'Yuhoooo!' called Baz. 'Get riding!'

Down swung the right feet and up lurched the front balls of the punch-riders at a tremendously steep angle. Sanchez leaned desperately forward to balance as the blue grass field shot away from them and then, still rising, they pivoted to the right and swooped over *Dragonfall 5* for a last wave.

'Oh golly!' thought Sanchez to himself.

In next to no time the floating field was lost against the darkness of space, and there were just the four of them rushing at over a hundred miles an hour through nothingness, the air tearing at their faces, the sun beating mercilessly down on them. The feeling of movement went right through them, and yet it was all in complete silence.

Tim loved it. He soon discovered by shouting questions that the punch-riders worked on two large magnets picking up the magnetic currents of the shattered planet and then working against each other. Not many people knew how to construct them nowadays so you had to make sure they lasted.

Perhaps an hour later Baz leaned forward and prodded Sanchez.

'Main pasture coming up below,' he called.

So Sanchez was just able to keep his seat when they lurched down almost headlong for hundreds of feet.

Below them, endlessly rippling and reaching as far into the bright blackness as you could see, was a great island of the floating blue grass, dotted with the countless herds of black and white cattle that were the pride of the Kench ranch.

'Swoosh!' the punch-riders swung for the last time beside a long line of fibreboard sheds.

'Yuhooo!' called the Kench brothers.

Sanchez got thankfully down on to fairly firm grass again.

Here, if they had not noticed this already, it was soon clear how important the two Kench brothers were, even though they were young. They introduced Tim and Sanchez in a very offhand way to their cattle boss, a short man with very strong arms called Rod, but they ignored all the other hired hands and rushed into a flurry of cattle-herding.

Before they began they lent Tim and Sanchez a punch-rider each.

'Treat 'em fair!' said Alec.

Then for hours and hours everyone worked, sorting out the cattle for branding and treatment of this cattle disease called brolick, killing dozens of the bulls that were not needed, then skinning the carcases, and salting and drying the meat.

By that time Sanchez could just about manage his punch-rider but Tim could soon do spin-turns, when you twist on the back ball and turn with the front.

Baz made them join in a competition in which each person was given just five minutes to herd as many cattle as possible into a rope square without using a dog. Baz could get twenty, and Rod could get twenty-eight, but even though Tim could do spin-turns the cattle just would not go where he wanted, and after five minutes there was not a single cow in the square.

The hired hands laughed and Sanchez could see that it was more than just a game. So when his turn came, he left his punch-rider, walked into the square and just called out, 'Cooooo up! Cooooo up!' clearly but not too loudly.

At first all the cows just pricked up their ears and snuffled. Then, slowly, as the seconds ticked away, some of them began to saunter towards the square.

Everyone watched astonished because, on the Broken World, you never called cattle, you drove them. But Sanchez had guessed that these cattle were descended from old Earth cattle, and had it in the blood to come to the old 'Cooooo up!' call.

No bulls came, but at the five-minute mark Sanchez had forty-five cows in the square, all looking puzzled and wondering why they had come.

After that the two boys could do no wrong.

'Man! Man!' said Rod wonderingly, 'you have the cattle lore and then some!'

Always the sun blazed away. Even when they came to eat they used the sun's rays, directed by mirrors to grill the great slabs of juicy, half-raw steaks which were what everyone always ate.

'And how's the Broken World strike you now?' asked Baz Kench as they lay digesting their steaks and getting ready to sleep.

'It's wonderful,' said Sanchez, and he meant it. 'The only thing I miss is night time. I wish it were dark now, and we were sitting around a camp fire watching the flames and the shadows.'

'Funny you should say that,' said Baz thoughtfully. 'That was what Uncle Richard said before he went away. "I'm going," he said, "to some place where I can sleep in darkness. That's a luxury I need." '

Tim and Sanchez forgot all their saddle sores and tiredness at the mention of Uncle Richard.

'You have an Uncle Richard?' asked Tim carefully.

'Did have!' laughed Baz. 'We weren't good enough for him. He said we were a pack of savages with no education. And I suppose he was some-ways right, but there weren't no call to laugh his own kinsfolk down. Anyways he left on a cargo space-boat three years ago for Earth. The Mother Planet he called it. Said the only place for a civilized man to live was a town called "Paris", and Paris is where he is.'

'I think then you ought to listen to this,' said Sanchez pulling the recording cylinder out of his pocket. 'I'm sorry we played it but we found it through one of your bulls charging at us.'

'Well nephews,' the cool, laughing voice of Uncle Richard began again and played right through. Baz and Alec drank in every word.

When it had finished Alec handled the cylinder and gave a half laugh.

'Do you know?' he said, 'this little old cylinder has made us lose sleep for the last three years! Ever since Uncle Richard up and awayed.'

' 'Fore he went,' continued Baz, 'he got a test ready for us. Said it would take the place of the education we didn't have. Gave us the first clue and said there were two more. The first to find all three clues got his old ranch, the Dorado Grand, and fifteen thousand head of cattle. Some prize! Trouble was we were so darned thick we couldn't make head nor tail of the first clue. So that's how far we got!'

'What was it?' asked Tim.

'I can recall every blamed word of it,' said Baz.

*'Covered over with sky*
*Hunters easily defy*
*Search in experience.'*

'How were we to make anything of that?'

'Try the first letters of each word,' said Tim quickly. 'The last one is a cheat because no real words begin with the letter X, but otherwise it's all right. COWSHEDSIX – Cowshed Six, and that's where we found it!'

The Kench brothers looked admiringly at Tim but said nothing, and just shook their heads.

'But why was it so important?' asked Sanchez. 'Whichever of you found it first it would still be in the Kench family.'

'We weren't going against each other!' said Baz in a shocked voice. 'It was those durned Maxwells! Uncle Richard married a Maxwell, and he gave them the first clue, same as us. Wouldn't have done to have Maxwells taking over the Dorado Grand. That's why we were all so steamed up!'

'Howsoever,' finished Alec, 'reckon the Maxwells were even worse educated than us! They never got anywhere with that first clue either or we should 'a heard of it.'

'But now, yuhooo!' shouted Baz leaping to his feet, 'thanks to you two and our little old bull we're away ahead. I'm off to get Dad on the radio and give him the news.' He hurried off to one of the sheds with an aerial on its roof.

'Isn't this the Kench ranch then?' asked Sanchez.

'This is just Main Pasture,' explained Alec. 'The homestead is away two hours ride off. That's where Dad is now. He leaves the cattle mostly to us nowadays. After we've slept some we'll ride you over, and show you we're not just hick cow-punchers, whatever Uncle Richard says. Here's the cylinder: you must show it to Dad yourself. You found it.'

Soon everyone was settled down in sleeping bags with hoods to screen them from the sun. They had had a hard time, and even the rolling of the grass under them, and the noises of the cattle could not keep Tim and Sanchez awake. They slept, and dreamed of cows and bulls, of punch-riders and floating islands in the sky.

## 2 · Ma Maxwell strikes

When they woke up it was almost like morning.
A patchy mist had risen out of the blue grass of
Main Pasture, their sleeping bags were damp
and there was a nip in the air.

Everyone was bustling for an early start back
to the Kench homestead, where Dad Kench
was eagerly waiting to hear the recording
cylinder. They chewed their meat cold and
dry, because there was no sun to grill steaks,
splashed their faces with mist water, and then
took their seats on the punch-riders.

Tim was such a good rider that he was given
his own but Sanchez was on the dog saddle of
Baz's punch-rider, because he wasn't really
good enough to drive for two hours across
empty space. He felt stiff and cold and not a
bit cheerful, but Baz and Alec were in a high
old humour over the finding of their first clue.

'Tuck your heels in, Sanch!' called Baz.

'Sun'll soon be shining again, and wait till you taste our home cooking! Get riding!'

'Yuhooo!' called Alec.

'Yuhoooo! Yiheeee!' called the hired hands.

Up shot the punch-riders into the mist. Cold, grey wetness enveloped them. Sanchez half shut his eyes against the moisture as they gathered speed. Briefly they shot through a gap of golden-sunlight, then mist closed in again.

Flop! something fell over Sanchez's head and shoulders. He heard Baz call out in the saddle behind him, then the something tightened about his arms and chest. There was a breathtaking jerk and he flew out of his saddle, upwards into the mist, kicking wildly.

As he dangled there in space he heard more shouts, lost and blurred in the grey vapour, then the distinct dull thud of a stunner being fired and a howl of pain that sounded like Baz. After this there was a chuckle above his head and no other noise, just a feeling that he was rushing furiously forwards, swinging sickeningly on the rope that had fallen over him.

After minutes of this blind race, the mist suddenly cleared and the sun was blazing out of the black sky once more. As he swung Sanchez could glimpse punch-riders all round him but he did not recognize any of the

cowboys riding them. Whatever was pulling him stopped.

'Up you come, my beauty!' said a very satisfied voice, and Sanchez was heaved slowly up to the punch-rider which had been pulling him.

A hand reached down to help him and he struggled astride the bar. As he did so he felt a hand reach into his side pocket and pull out the recording cylinder. There was a whoop of triumph from his captor.

'Got the clue right here, Danull!' he called. 'Knew we'd picked the right one.'

'What happened to Baz Kench?' shouted Danull, who was the rider to Sanchez's left. 'I heard you fire.'

'Stunner in the left shoulder,' called his captor in a grim, satisfied voice. 'He won't be herding cattle for a week or two!'

'Good for you, Lee!' called Danull, and the other riders in earshot gave whoops and cheers.

'Now, home fast, while they're still turning circles in the cloud,' ordered Sanchez's captor, who seemed to be called Lee. 'And wrap your legs round if you don't want to swing at the rope's end!' he hissed in Sanchez's ear. 'You called on the Kenchs, and now you can set things even and pay a call on the Maxwells.'

He chuckled again, swooped his punch-rider hard to the right and accelerated straight into top speed.

The flight seemed to last hours. Poor Sanchez was very uncomfortable sitting astride the bar with the rope lasso tight around his arms, and he was also very unhappy.

They had been ambushed in the clouds and he had fallen right into the hands of the rival Maxwells with the vital second clue. Baz was injured and where was Tim? How had the Maxwells known what was going on?

The flight ended at last. A jagged hunk of rock like a small mountain appeared against the dark sky. A few, low-spreading trees grew on the rock, and floating away from its surface but anchored to it by a heavy chain was a ramshackle bunch of brown fibreboard rooms.

The raiding party swung around these with the usual whooping and shouting which was answered by cheering and calling from down below. The escorting punch-riders peeled off to the lower rooms but Lee and Danull swooped down to land on the broad verandah of the topmost room which floated a clear hundred feet above the rock surface of the little asteroid.

Sanchez promptly tumbled off the bar on to the floor, from where he could see Lee Maxwell, his captor, for the first time.

Lee was only two years older than he was and Danull was about Sanchez's age. Lee had a lean sharp face and foxy blue eyes; Danull looked heavy and good-natured. The two stood there, laughing down at him, slapping each other's backs.

'Will you look who's dropped in on us!' said Lee.

'Soon made himself at home, hasn't he?' said Danull.

'Picked him off the saddle like a ripe plum,' boasted Lee.

'Think they're the only folk on Broken World

with a radio receiver,' Danull jeered. 'That'll larn 'em to boast too soon to old Dad Kench!'

'Lee! Danull!' a firm woman's voice boomed out of the open door on to the verandah. 'Quit funnin' and bring him in here!'

Instantly Lee and Danull's faces grew serious. They picked Sanchez up and half carried, half walked him out of the sunlight into a big, bare room. Seated in a chair like a small throne was a grim old lady with silver hair and a jaw like a nut cracker. She was glaring at Sanchez but he could only look at the tall fair-haired boy standing behind her.

'Dave Anderson!' he gasped. 'What are you doing here?'

It was his old enemy from their school days on the Empty Planet last year. He and Dave had never liked each other from the first day they met on the school playing field.

'Might have known it was you!' Dave scowled back. 'Always snooping about stirring up trouble.'

'Might have known I'd find you here,' retorted Sanchez, 'with a bunch of kidnappers!'

'Keep a civil tongue in your head, boy, or I'll have you dropped in the Glory Hole to learn your manners,' snapped the old lady. 'I'm Ma Maxwell. I take no cheek from my own boys, and I certainly take no cheek from no one else's! Cousin Dave is a Maxwell on his mother's side, and we're proud to have some education in the family at last.'

'He wasn't much good at anything but jet polo when I was in school with him,' said Sanchez spitefully.

'That does it!' roared the old lady. 'Ma Maxwell doesn't threaten twice. Into the Glory Hole with him, boys! Then hand over that recording cylinder, and let's hear what tarnation nonsense your uncle wants us to get up to next.'

And before Sanchez could say 'Dragonfall,' Dave had opened a trapdoor in the floor, and Lee and Danull had popped him down it with a firm push to counter the lack of gravity.

Down a wooden chute he swooshed, feet first through another trap to land with a gentle bump on a smelly pile of drying cattle skins in a room crammed with the junk of ages, with no windows and one locked door.

'Hmpf!' thought Sanchez. 'There's one woman who knows her own mind!'

With no one to bother him it did not take him long to wriggle out of the lasso that Lee had dropped over him, but there seemed no way to get out of the Glory Hole. He did not expect to be left there for long so he decided that the most irritating thing he could do was to go to sleep. And that was what he did, on a broken old sofa.

He had not been long asleep before he was roused by Ma Maxwell's foot prodding him in the ribs. She certainly was irritated about something.

'So this is the space-bum who'll cheat my boys out of the Dorado Grand, is it?' she shouted.

'We didn't cheat,' protested Sanchez, scrambling to his feet. 'It was a competition.'

'Competition!' she snorted. 'Well, will you tell me how this cylinder came to be in your pocket when Uncle Richard particularly says it is to be put back where you found it?'

'But the bull broke the shed,' Sanchez spluttered rather weakly.

'A likely tale,' Ma Maxwell said. 'On your way, young man! We're taking you back to those swindling Kenchs where you belong. And when I see old Dad Kench I shall personally tell him what I think of his methods.'

Sanchez found himself blinking in the sunlight at the top of a long rope ladder down which he and Ma Maxwell began to climb. Below them the whole Maxwell ranch seemed to be gathered with dozens of punch-riders.

Ma Maxwell herself wore a splendid leather divided skirt, a padded blouse, and a crash helmet with a big floppy sun brim, and when she got to the bottom of the ladder she was puffing a little.

She had a special double punch-rider with a broad canvas seat slung between the two poles. As she got on to it all the hired hands fell quiet, and Lee motioned Sanchez on to a dog saddle which he had fitted to his rider.

'Men!' roared Ma Maxwell, 'we're going to the Kench ranch in strength because that's the only fitting way for a Maxwell to go anywheres!'

There was a shout of approval and a slapping of stunner belts.

'But!' her great voice cut in, 'I only want trouble if I ask for it, and if anyone makes trouble without my say-so, I'll have his hide! Is that understood?'

There was a silence in the sun, only disturbed by the creaking of the brown fibreboard floors chained above them. Danull winked at Sanchez.

'Right,' called Ma Maxwell, 'get riding!' and with a tremendous yodelling and shouting the whole Maxwell clan took off skywards led by Ma Maxwell's billowing double punch-rider.

Round the ranch they circled, then off at full speed in a great V-shape like geese. Sanchez wondered whether he would ever get used to the angle of climb and the tearing air.

This ride did not end as suddenly as the others had done. The Kench ranch showed up white and clear from miles away. No trees grew on the limestone of the asteroid, and the house itself was lime-washed pure white, though it too floated in a chain of rooms above the surface of the rock.

The whooping and yippeeing of the Maxwells brought figures hurrying out from everywhere, and when Ma Maxwell landed on a flattened square below the house at least a hundred armed cowboys, including Alec and Tim, were gathered about a very grand old man in black moleskin with a huge, silver-handled stunner in his belt.

Ignoring everyone else, Ma Maxwell shouldered her way towards the old man, her leather skirts flapping.

'Stand from about me!' she roared magnificently. 'It's you I've come to see, Lou Kench, and not your minions. Can't you stand up without them to support you?'

'I may be old,' said the old man in a gentle voice, 'but I am not deaf, Liza Maxwell, nor have I time to waste listening to you. State your business, and then go with the rest of your uninvited tribe.'

'I've brought you two things,' said Ma Maxwell, just as loudly as before. 'One,' she pointed her finger at Sanchez, 'and two,' she threw the recording cylinder at the old man's

feet. 'You might as well keep it, since your boys cheated by taking it from the place where it was meant to be left. But I've come to tell you, Lou Kench, that from now on it's war!'

A muttering broke out from the crowd gathered in the blazing sun. Ma Maxwell glared around her and the muttering died away.

'It's war,' she repeated. 'I mean my boys

to find those next two clues and to have the Dorado Grand for themselves. If Uncle Richard was blamed fool enough to hide clues in Condavee Country then to Condavee Country my boys will go and get what's theirs. And I defy a skulking, white Condavee to stop 'em! And what's more, Lou Kench, if you and your thieving sons know what's good for them they'll keep away from Condavee Country and keep away from my boys!'

She stopped. The old man, who had turned white with rage, just called out one word: 'Baz!' he called.

From the door of the white room immediately above them Baz Kench stepped out on to the verandah. He looked pale, and his left arm was in a sling. Another murmur swept over the crowd.

'That's what your sons have done already to one of my boys,' said the old man. 'Maxwell blood is bad blood. Always was, always will be. The Kenchs are in the race for the Dorado Grand and the Kenchs will win it!

'Now!' he continued, 'I'll give you a count of ten. By the end of that time if you and your pack haven't cleared my homestead I'll pepper the lot of you!'

The two old people glared at each other,

while everywhere hands reached for stunners.

'One,' said Dad Kench quietly.

'Two.'

Ma Maxwell threw back her head and laughed. 'Didn't know you could count so far!' she roared. 'The first Kench to have an education, and the last!'

She strode back to her punch-rider and pushed her feet into the stirrup slings.

'Three. Four. Five,' Dad Kench continued.

'I invite you all,' the old woman called out, 'to the Maxwell's house-warming party at the Dorado Grand. That's if Baz and Alec get out of Condavee Country alive!' She laughed again.

'Six. Seven. Eight,' Dad Kench counted on.

'Get riding!' Ma Maxwell bellowed, and shot straight up in her canvas seat. All about her with deafening shouts of 'Yippee!' and 'Yuhoo,' the Maxwells rose up on their punch-riders.

Twice they swept around the white Kench homestead in a rising circle, jeering and calling. Then they shot away in a great V and were soon lost in the blackness of Space.

Only Sanchez was left where the crowd had been. Old Dad Kench looked at him and smiled.

'You're welcome,' he said.

## 3 · Condavee Country

Five hours later, Tim, Sanchez, Baz and Alec were closing in on Condavee Country.

Baz had a stiff shoulder from Lee Maxwell's stunner, and Sanchez was very wobbly at steering his own punch-rider, but they had agreed that to move fast and with a small party was their best chance.

Sparrer had been sent back to Old Elias with a mercury flask and a piece of stressed tungsten which Tim had thought might do to mend *Dragonfall 5*.

Sanchez had washed and eaten and told of his imprisonment in the Glory Hole, and then, without fuss, Dad Kench had seen them off.

'Do your best,' he had said, 'and if those Condavees catch sight of you drive back here like lickety spit. They haven't got no punch-riders, praise be!'

Now Condavee Country was looming up

huge and jagged out of space as they rode in cautiously on its dark side.

Condavee Country was the biggest chunk left of the Broken World. Fifty miles square, so Baz told them, its red rock cut deeply by canyons and gullies, and green with plants and trees, it was riddled with the caves and passages where the white Condavee savages lived.

It did not spin round as a planet does. One side always faced the sun and one side, the side they were approaching now, was always in shadow, although it was not really dark.

As they swooped down in single file into a huge canyon brimming with forest, harsh bird cries came up to them, and from somewhere deep in the red mountain came a low musical twanging sound, as if someone were plucking at the strings of an enormous harp, very slowly.

'Hark at 'em!' whispered Baz, 'murdering savages!'

'What exactly do the Condavees do?' asked Tim, who liked to be exact.

'Nobody knows,' replied Baz solemnly, 'because nobody comes here. 'Tisn't safe; they're not civilized.'

Sanchez thought the Condavees must be very dreadful to be less civilized than Ma Maxwell and her Glory Hole, but he did not say anything. They sank quietly to rest in the half darkness where the shadow forest crept up to a jutting spur of the canyon side.

'We'll leave the punch-riders here under this overhang,' said Baz, 'then scout in the shadow forest until we know where we are.'

'Hullo!' said Alec, and whistled softly, 'will you look who's here before us!'

There, under the overhanging rock, were parked three punch-riders, marked with the double M brand of the Maxwells. Lee, Danull and Dave were ahead of them! There was no time to lose.

Quickly they heaved their punch-riders down to the forest and left them hidden under the fleshy leaves of a tree whose branches reached like arms in the green twilight. Walking was fairly easy because there was a bit of gravity on such a big asteroid.

'Twaing! twoing!' Again the distant, plucked

55

notes vibrated from the rock and the sharp bird cries rose from the shadow forest.

'Uncle Richard must have been turned in the head to lead us down here,' whispered Alec, looking nervously about him. 'Everything's green: green leaves, green grass; 'tisn't natural, and no sunlight.'

But Sanchez was enjoying the shade and he had not been brought up in a place where all the grass was blue. Something was stirring in the treetops and he was straining to see what it was. Then, under a broad leaf like a four-fingered hand, a small face peeped out.

'Wazzat?' said Baz reaching for his stunner.

'Monkeys!' said Sanchez happily, and scrambled up the branches to get nearer to them.

Monkeys they were, a whole band of them, small black monkeys, with white necks and grey patches around their big black eyes.

They looked at the boys and the boys looked up at them.

'Some of them seem to be holding something,' said Sanchez, climbing back to the ground with green lichen all over his space suit, 'but I couldn't quite see what it was.'

'Come on,' said Baz, 'we're way behind those durned Maxwells already!'

They threaded their way warily between the

trees, making for the towering rocks at the end of the canyon. Above them the monkeys leapt excitedly from tree to tree, chattering shrilly, with now and then a light, musical pinging noise, which the boys could not understand. The underground harp noise which they had first heard was silent now.

Though the forest was in everlasting shadow, it was warm and they soon stopped to drink water from their flasks and eat some dried meat and biscuits. Sanchez scrambled up another finger tree to meet the monkeys again. The others, silent, sat chewing at its foot, for the Kenchs were not a bit happy away from their blue grass pastures.

A few minutes later Sanchez called down very softly. 'Don't make any noise or sudden movement as I climb down, but just see what I've got!'

Very gently he came down the tree. Perched on his shoulder, eating a piece of his biscuit with one hand, was a tiny black monkey. It was looking at the boys with just as much interest as they were looking at it. But the really remarkable thing about it was that in its other hand it was holding a miniature harp.

'Musical monkeys!' gasped Tim. 'So that was the noise we heard.'

It was a very simple harp, just a bent piece of wood with three wires drawn across it, but the monkey calmly proved what it was by striking two high notes on it and then, after a pause, a low note.

'Well that's the durndest critter!' said Baz,

smiling for the first time since they entered the shadow forest. 'Strike me if it isn't the image of our Auntie Sara! Do you think they're good to eat?'

'Twoing!' the little monkey struck another sharp note and gave Baz a very old-fashioned look. Several more 'twoings!' answered it from up in the branches.

'You want to be very careful what you say in front of strange animals,' said Sanchez severely. 'We've often found animals that could understand lots that we said even though they couldn't speak.'

Muttering about 'Condavee witch-tricks', Baz and Alec led the way on towards the high rocks. Tim and Sanchez lagged behind, admiring the monkey, which still perched on Sanchez's shoulder while its friends followed above. As a result they were yards behind when they rounded the last tree and found themselves at the end of the forest.

Ahead, in the cliff face, was a dark cave mouth. Standing in the cave mouth with their backs to them, quite unawares, were Lee, Danull and Dave Anderson. They held stunners in their hands. So too did Baz and Alec, and what was more they had raised them and were just about to stun their rivals without warning.

For a vital second Tim and Sanchez were too surprised to act. Then, just as Baz's finger was squeezing the trigger, the monkey acted instead.

'Doin-n-ng!'

Even though he saw the monkey pull the wire, the high pitched note made Sanchez jump, and it made their enemies duck for cover and Baz and Alec jerk just as they fired.

'Pthud! Pthud!' Patches of rock dust flew as the stunner rays struck the cave wall. Lee and Danull leapt into the darkness. Dave turned and fired his stunner once, knocking Alec's crash helmet flying, before he too dived into the cave. Baz and Alec rushed in after them firing wildly.

'Come on!' shouted Tim. The monkey jumped chattering for a tree branch. Tim and Sanchez followed the others into the dark.

'Pthud! Pthud!' more stunner rays struck the walls, 'pthud!'

'There they go!' came Baz's voice. There was the clump clump of hurrying feet, then sudden, complete silence.

'They're this way!' called Alec somewhere to the right. They heard his footsteps running into the dark. Again, very suddenly, they cut short.

'Hold on, Alec!' shouted Baz, firing three stunner bolts quickly. 'I'm come. . . .'

His voice cut off in the middle of a word. Tim and Sanchez were alone in the cavern. Just a little light came from the entrance.

'Click!' Tim, always ready for trouble, switched on his torch.

'Perhaps they've fallen down a hole,' he said. 'Stay here, Sanchez, while I go and look. Don't move!'

'Don't you worry,' said Sanchez firmly, 'I won't!'

Tim set off down the cave. He turned a corner but the light of his torch still showed.

'Look out!' his voice came back, suddenly shrill, 'it's the Conda . . .' Again there was silence. The light had gone.

'. . . vees,' finished Sanchez, 'and if you don't mind I'll come quietly.'

Around the corner where Tim had vanished came two broad-shouldered men, one of whom was holding Tim's torch. They wore white floppy trousers and white tunics, their faces also were pale, but their hair was black, and they wore neat golden collars. They bowed politely to Sanchez.

'People who feed hungry monkeys never have sacks put over their heads,' said one of them. 'I will introduce. I am Hol See Ran,' (he said each bit of his name distinctly), 'and this is my brother, Hol Van Ser.'

'I'm San Chez,' said Sanchez, who had been looking forward to meeting the Condavees ever since he had found the musical monkeys.

'If you follow us,' said Hol See Ran, 'holding your light-stick, we will bring you to your cross friends.'

He smiled, Sanchez took Tim's torch, and the march through the dark began. Sometimes they heard stumbling and grumbling ahead of them, but they never caught up with the others.

Sanchez chatted busily. He learned that the monkeys had been passing messages about them by harp notes to the Condavees ever since they landed in the canyon. But the big, deep harp notes were not messages.

'Those are for pleasure,' said Hol Van Ser. 'We make music in the Great Cave. But we like the monkeys to make music too. With the Condavees everything is music. Monkeys make many bad notes!' He pulled a face.

'Is the Great Cave where the beautiful carvings are?' asked Sanchez, remembering Uncle Richard's message.

Hol See Ran and Hol Van Ser looked knowingly at each other.

'Your Uncle Rich Ard has been before you,' said Hol Van Ser.

'He's not my uncle,' said Sanchez.

'Pity,' said Hol Van Ser, 'he is a good man,

enjoys music, feeds monkeys, never cross.' They all laughed.

Soon they came out into the twilight of a great terrace cut deeply into the rock, looking out on to space, but still on the shadow side. Here everyone was having the sacks, which had shut them up so quickly, pulled from their heads, and a row of Condavees was sitting quietly in chairs watching.

Lee came out of his sack looking very flustered and in a terrible temper.

'Take me to your leader!' he shouted.

All the Condavees laughed. One of them, who was stroking a monkey that sat on his arm, got up smiling and walked over to Sanchez.

'The Condavees have no leaders,' he said, 'but for this week I am Master of the Music. I am Beel Dal Az. You will introduce us?'

Beel Dal Az and Sanchez walked down the rumpled line.

'Tim, Lee, Baz, Al Ek, Dan Ull,' Sanchez introduced in turn until he came to his old school enemy. 'Day Vuh An Der Son,' he said very distinctly.

'Very long name,' said the Master of the Music gravely.

'Very long name, very little sense,' said

Sanchez with a straight face. Dave was furious but he did not dare say anything.

'You,' said the Master, pointing to the Maxwells and Dave, 'shoot monkeys. You,' he pointed to the Kenchs, 'feed monkeys.'

He paused to let this sink in.

'There,' he continued, waving to the edge of the terrace, 'are your punch-riders. Anyone who wishes to go will do so now. The rest will sit down.'

Everyone sat down. Dave began to comb his hair. Somewhere, in the rock but very close now, the great harp began to play again, a slow sad tune that shivered in the air.

'We, the Condavee savages,' began Beel Dal Az with a smile, 'are glad to welcome the nephews of Rich Ard Kench and their friends. You come to find the third clue in your hunt. Also your uncle wished you to come to see that we are not savages as you suppose. We are white because we live out of the sun. We do not eat cow meat as you do. We think that all of life is for pleasure, not to shoot each other with stunners like savages.'

Here he paused and looked rather grim. Baz blushed a little.

'You will see the carvings of the Great Cave,' went on Beel Dal Az, 'you will eat with us, you will wash up, then you will say which you think is the most beautiful carving. If you choose right you take the third clue. If you choose wrong for you the race is over. Afterwards you will sleep here and then, as friends, you will go.'

'How many guesses do we get at the most beautiful carving?' asked Dave Anderson.

'Not guesses, choices,' said Beel Dal Az. 'Four choices, one to each nephew, none to you, none to Tim, none to San Chez. Now we will go.'

He clapped his hands. Laughing and talking, with harps and little trumpets playing, a whole crowd of the Condavees and the boys walked down a dark corridor. The twanging of the great, hidden harp grew louder until they turned into a vast hall lit by long, deep windows in the rock.

'The Great Cave,' said Tim, looking at the carvings ranged around the walls.

'I like the shadow forest better,' said Sanchez.

'Some harp!' said Baz watching a group of Condavees pull at the great wires that stretched from roof to floor all along one wall.

'Dark old hole!' said Lee, who was secretly rather impressed.

Beel Dal Az made them walk right around

the room looking at all fifty carvings. Some were of people in robes and crowns, some were of animals fighting or pulling chariots. A great deal of hard work had been put into carving all the detail of the soft, red rock.

'And now to eat!' said Beel Dal Az, when they were all looking rather lost. The music burst out again with Beel Dal Az conducting it and they all went back to the terrace where the Condavee women were waiting with a four-course banquet for forty people.

There was of course, a musical background. At the end of the terrace a big bowl of water was heating over a charcoal fire.

First there was a clear vegetable soup.

'Pappymash!' snorted Alec.

Then there was a chestnut bake with mixed nut dressing and vegetables.

'Now I feel I got something in my innards,' said Danull.

Then there was avocado pie with herb stuffing and sharp cream.

'That was kind of tasty,' said Lee patting his stomach.

Lastly there were jungle fruit fritters in chocolate mousse.

'I don't know that I've eaten better,' said Baz.

'Now you will wash up,' said Beel Dal Az. 'All things give pleasure if they are properly done! Clean hot water, warm dry cloths, fine round bowls. It will give harmony to your minds. Then you will choose.'

One hundred and sixty bowls later the boys could see what he meant. Even washing up is pleasant if you do it properly. They had seven stacks of round, shining bowls in front of them.

'Almost like picking apples,' said Sanchez.

'My hands are all wrinkled and nasty,' said Dave.

Then back they went to the Great Cave. Hundreds of Condavees followed them in excitedly to see them try to choose the most beautiful statue.

'If you choose wrongly,' said Beel Dal Az, 'you will hear this noise.'

'Boiing!' a deep, groaning harp-string twanged.

'If you choose rightly you will hear this.'

'Ooooom!' a long, golden note sounded out.

'Take your time, take advice and counsel. If your taste is bad you will never have the Dorado Grand but you may still be happy. Life is full of surprises!' He turned smiling to look for more music.

Round and round the boys walked, brooding

and talking, the Kenchs and the Maxwells keeping well apart. Baz was very impressed by a carving of a king and queen riding on an elephant.

'They've even got the jewels in her crown!' he said.

Alec liked the one of three frantic men trying to hold back three wild horses.

'Look at them muscles!' he said.

But Sanchez felt that a small simple statue of a naked boy playing a harp and laughing as he played was quite different from the others and much more likely to be the one to go for.

'It ain't decent,' said Baz. 'Where's his clothes? Would you play a harp sitting in your altogether?'

Finally they all drifted back to where Beel Dal Az was conducting a small orchestra and told him they were as ready as they would ever be. He clapped his hands for silence.

Sanchez stared unhappily out through the long windows at the dark skies of space. He was sure Baz and Alec wcre wrong. The Condavees admired simple things and music.

Lee chose first. Biting his lips nervously he strode forward and put his hand on the statue of a huge man wrestling with a writhing snake.

'Boiing!' the groaning note sounded. He had lost. A hum of talk went round the room.

Baz stepped forward next. He was sweating with anxiety but he marched grimly up to the king and queen on the elephant.

'Thus un!' he said.

'Boiing!' the second failure.

The good-natured Danull came out to make the last choice for the Maxwells; Dave Anderson was whispering urgently to him.

Danull walked uncertainly down a row, then walked back a few steps, then pointed miserably to the statue of three men drinking around a loaded table.

'Boiing!' the last hope of the Maxwells had gone. Now the room was very tense. Even Beel Dal Az had stopped smiling.

'It's the boy with the harp!' whispered Sanchez desperately to Alec, 'I know it is! Choose that one.'

But Alec walked down towards the three men and the three horses. He stopped by it. Somehow the feeling of how the Condavees were reacting was wrong. He caught some of them looking shocked. Oh well! he might as well give Sanchez's hunch a try out.

Alec clip-clopped down to the statue of the boy with the harp.

'I suppose it ain't decent,' he said, 'but at least he looks cheerful! I'll choose this one.'

'Ooooom!' sounded the golden note for success, but it was almost lost in the cheering. Even Danull congratulated the Kenchs. Only Lee and Dave looked very black as they muttered in a corner.

'Too much excitement is bad for the brain,' said Beel Dal Az. 'First you will sleep. Then you will take the third clue from behind the statue and hear your Uncle Rich Ard's message. Then we say goodbye.'

It was hopeless to argue with the Master of the Music and, in fact, they were very tired. They were each shown into a dark bedroom with cool linen bedclothes and soon specially low harp music sent them to sleep.

# 4 · Scientists are useful

Tim woke up with a distinct feeling that something was wrong. When he got a feeling like
that he was usually right.

He got up and put on the horrid space suit
Big Mother had made them wear, then he
woke Sanchez and Baz and Alec. Next he
peeped into Dave Anderson's room. The bed
had not been slept in. The two Maxwell
brothers had not slept in their beds either.

Tim hurried out on to the terrace where Hol
See Ran and Hol Van Ser were sitting listening
to music. They did not know that the Maxwells
had left but their punch-riders had gone.

'Perhaps they are sad that you won the
third clue,' suggested Hol Van Ser. 'They
leave to hide their sadness. Perhaps the Master
of the Music knows.'

'Where is he?' asked Tim.

'He digs in a distant garden,' said Hol Van

Ser. 'Even digging gives pleasure if it is well done.'

'He's more likely to be teaching the monkeys to play harps!' said Tim, rather rudely because he was getting very worried. 'Do you mind if we go along to pick up the third clue now?'

'What do you think is wrong?' asked Sanchez as they hurried down the corridor to the Great Cave.

'You don't think those thieving Maxwells have stolen the third clue, do you?' asked Baz strapping on his stunner belt.

'When Dave Anderson is about anything can happen,' snapped Tim.

The Great Cave was empty, for once the huge harp was silent.

'The third clue is kept on the shelf behind the most beautiful statue,' said Hol Van Ser. 'I know because I dust here, where even to dust gives pleasure.'

'It's gone!' said Tim, 'I knew it! Serves us right for taking things easily.'

'Goldurned, cattle-hogging, saddle-biting, dusty-nosed sons of turnips!' roared Baz. 'Wait till I get my hands on them!'

'They're hours ahead of us,' said Alec, 'they may have the last clue by now.'

The Condavees were particularly upset

because they could not imagine anyone wanting to break rules.

'Just a minute,' said Tim when everyone was complaining and shouting, 'let's get one thing straight. They've cheated, haven't they, really cheated?'

'Too true they have,' shouted Baz.

'Right,' said Tim crisply, 'now you shall see science to the rescue. We are going to cheat too, and dreadfully! How long will it take us to ride back to *Dragonfall 5*?'

'Three hours or thereabouts,' said Baz. 'Come on, if you've got an idea, let's get moving!'

'Oh there's no hurry,' said Tim, 'we've all the time in the world.' But irritatingly he would not tell them his plan.

They said goodbye to the Condavees, though Beel Dal Az was still away digging, and soared away from the terrace.

Soon Condavee Country was just a rocky ball against the blackness of space, the sun was beating down on them, the wind whistled by their ears and the blue grass pastures rippled away below them. On and on they rode till Sanchez was saddle-sore, and their faces were sun blistered.

At last they swooped down on *Dragonfall 5*

floating lonely, blue and black and silver against the dark sky. No whoops and yippees this time. Baz and Alec were grim and sad at the thought of being cheated out of the Dorado Grand.

Big Mother was delighted to see them back.

'Knitting's finished and I've nothing to read,' she said, and even Old Elias looked cheerful. Jerk licked everybody.

Big Mother and Old Elias listened to all that had happened. Big Mother was very angry when she heard about Sanchez being dropped in the Glory Hole.

'Wait till I see that woman!' she said, and they both looked serious when they heard how the Maxwells had cheated.

'But now we're going to cheat,' said Tim. '*Dragonfall* is repaired now, isn't she?'

'Tungsten wasn't super-stressed,' said Old Elias, 'but it'll hold.'

'We're going back in time,' said Tim smugly.

'How so?' asked Baz suspiciously.

'Well,' explained Tim, 'of course *Dragonfall 5* can go faster than light. All starships can. If you go faster than light you go faster than time because light is the same as time.'

Old Elias nodded but the Kenchs looked very blank.

'I mean,' continued Tim, 'the Battle of Hastings is still going on somewhere in space, you've just got to go fast enough to get back to it. People don't do it much because it's a strain on ships and pilots, but we only want to go back twelve hours to the time of our four-course banquet.'

'Oh, I get it,' said Sanchez. 'We nip back to the Great Cave at a time when it was empty and the third clue was still in its place, and we take it!'

'Not quite,' said Tim. 'We can't take it because the Maxwells took it and you can't alter time. We just listen to Uncle Richard's message, wipe it out and record a false one, and send the Maxwells off on a fool's errand.'

'Bingo!' yelled Sanchez and they all gave Tim a cheer. Scientists are useful.

For a while Tim and Old Elias fiddled about with arithmetic tables and slide rules, working out the loop in space and the speed they would need to get back to Condavee Country twelve hours ago. Soon they were ready and the circuits for the rocket motors were heating up.

The cabin was crammed full because they had brought the punch-riders in. Everyone was very excited at the idea of tricking Dave

Anderson. The old starship hummed and shivered as the rocket fuels mixed themselves. Old Elias bent over the controls and Tim sat in the co-pilot's seat.

Five, four, three, two, one, zero! For a second *Dragonfall 5* hesitated, tilting back on to her tail. Then, in a blaze of light, the rocket pods surged power and she went storming up into the dark heavens.

'Some ton-up!' breathed Baz. Sanchez felt very proud.

Twenty thousand, fifty thousand, eighty thousand, their speed rose.

'Rocket power off! Star-drive on!' called Old Elias. Tim slipped over the lever to star-drive. The shrill whine rose, grey mist of interspace swept about the cabin windows, faster than light, faster than time, *Dragonfall 5* swept about in a great curve, every rivet on her sides straining. Tim pored over his stop watch.

'Four seconds, three seconds, two seconds, out . . . out!' he called and, with a gentle 'pop' sound, *Dragonfall 5* came off star-drive and into the blackness of real space again. But her star-drive was always going wrong. Where had it landed them?

'We've made it,' called Sanchez happily, 'Condavee Country sunside is just below us!'

Quickly they got out their punch-riders and coasted gently down to the rocky sides of the big asteroid. They had to be careful because they didn't want to meet themselves! They could hear the banquet going on down the terrace as they drove quietly up to the windows of the Great Cave.

'Wonder which course we're eating?' whispered Sanchez.

Leaving the punch-riders clamped to the rock, they climbed down into the Great Cave. No one was there. Behind the boy-with-the-harp statue lay Uncle Richard's recording cylinder – the third clue.

'Quick!' said Tim, 'I reckon they're round to the fruit fritters! We've no time to lose.' He clicked on the recording cylinder.

'Well, nephews,' Uncle Richard's self-satisfied voice sounded again, 'if you have got this far you are much wiser and more tasteful than you were when you started.'

'You can say that again!' muttered Baz.

'See that in future you never call the Condavees savages,' Uncle Richard's voice lectured away. 'The title deeds to Dorado Grand are held by the Hermit of the Hollow Hill.'

Baz and Alec groaned as they heard this.

'Handle him with great care, he is a

remarkable old man and he has a great truth to tell you. Use the Dorado Grand wisely, and think of me sometimes here in Paris living life as it should be lived. Goodbye, dear savages, and good luck!' There was a mocking laugh and the record was finished.

'Dad durn and drat it!' fumed Baz. 'First he sends us off to these Condavee savages, then he sends us off to that pesky old cattle thief at Hollow Hill.'

'But the Condavees aren't savages,' protested Sanchez, 'that's why he sent us here, to find out. Probably this Hermit is a nice old man. Where is Hollow Hill?'

'It's a little old asteroid, the shape of a saucer, about an hour's ride from our homestead,' explained Alec. 'This old fellow lives there on what he grows and the cattle he steals from us!'

'Never mind now,' said Tim, 'we'll be in here soon to choose that statue and we can't meet ourselves. I've wiped out all the last half of the recording, so who is going to add the false bit?'

'I will!' said Sanchez eagerly, 'I know just what to say,' and he did too, in an almost perfect imitation of Uncle Richard's superior voice.

'I have hidden the title deeds, dear nephews,' Sanchez imitated, 'in the dirtiest place I know of, the Glory Hole in my sister-in-law's ranch. Search in the rubbish which that slipshod woman collects and you will find what you deserve. Goodbye, dear nephews.'

As Sanchez ended they all burst into helpless laughter.

'If we could only see Ma Maxwell's face when she hears that!' spluttered Baz.

'The place'll get cleaned out at last!' said Alec.

'Think of Dave scrabbling about in all those smelly cattle skins!' said Sanchez.

'Listen!' said Tim, who never laughed as much as the others. 'I can hear trumpets, the banquet's over. Everyone will be here in a minute. Out through the window!'

As the doors opened they scrambled out of the window to their punch-riders, just escaping the difficult situation of meeting themselves twelve hours earlier. Time is an odd thing. It does not do to get too muddled up in it.

They were soon back in *Dragonfall 5* telling Big Mother what they had done. She did not laugh quite as much as they expected.

'Hmmmm!' she said, when Sanchez told her how he had imitated Uncle Richard, 'I just hope it works out all right.'

'Well,' said Old Elias, 'where do we make for now, twelve hours ahead?'

'Yes,' said Baz, 'let's get back to our right time and somewhere just between our homestead and the Maxwell ranch. That's where Hollow Hill lies.'

Back they went.

Five, four, three, two, one, zero! *Dragonfall 5* went thundering back to the proper time twelve hours ahead, where they really belonged.

This time they did not pop out of star-drive at exactly the right spot. But they could just see the little asteroid of Hollow Hill floating in space about three or four miles away. They decided to travel the last bit by punch-rider.

'And we'd better go easy,' warned Baz. 'The Hermit don't welcome visitors. Blew the last lot to kingdom come!'

Big Mother waved goodbye as they set off, and then quickly started some new knitting to stop herself worrying.

# 5 · Real neighbourly

Hollow Hill was just a bowl of rock, half a mile across. In the middle was a stone hut, and round the hut were patches of corn and potatoes, and low, droopy fruit trees. It looked very lonely. The sun beat down on it and the wind blew over it.

Very cautiously the four boys landed their punch-riders at the edge of the bowl and looked nervously across at the silent stone hut.

'Anyone at home?' called Baz.

But there was no answer.

Slowly, trying to look all ways at once, they walked through the orchards and vegetable patches. Sanchez was greedier than the others and he got left behind quite a way because he found a tree loaded with nectarine plums. No one noticed. The others reached the Hermit's pigsties.

Alec sniffed. 'He don't clean 'em out any too often,' he said.

'Duck!' shouted Baz, and as he shouted he

hurled himself forward, knocking Tim flying into the dust. The most tremendous bolt of crackly blue light flew over their heads.

Behind them, holding a huge, old-fashioned stunner ray, was an old man who had just popped up from behind the pigsties. A long wire trailed back from his stunner ray to a portable electric generator.

He looked furious all over his brown face.

'Clear off my land!' he roared, his grizzled beard wagging, 'or you'll get a bolt up the backside!' With another great sizzle of

electricity, he fired again, just over their heads. Behind him the three boys could see Sanchez creeping up. The old man had not noticed him.

'But we've come to see you,' said Baz.

'I don't want to see anybody,' the Hermit shouted. 'Why do you think I live out here if I have to. . . .'

'Phut!'

Sanchez had hurled his throwing knife clean through the wire from the old man's stunner ray. With a blue flash it went dead. The Hermit glared at him helplessly, then threw down the stunner.

'Creeping up on me like that!' he said. 'You ought to know better!'

'Look,' said Baz, getting to his feet, 'we've come from Uncle Richard. He said he knew you and that you had the title deeds to the Dorado Grand.'

'From Richard Kench, is it?' asked the old man, squinting at them suspiciously.

'Yes, I'm Baz Kench, this is my brother Alec, and these are two friends of ours.'

'Humph!' said the Hermit, looking at Sanchez, 'ruined a length of wire!'

Sanchez was bothered if he was going to say 'sorry'. They stared awkwardly at each other.

'Tell you what,' said the Hermit slyly, 'now you're here I'll make you some coffee. But while I'm doing it, how about weeding this patch of sweet corn for me? I'm an old man and stiff with bending.'

The patch of corn looked enormous but they could not very well say no. The Hermit had gone inside his stone hut. Tim and Sanchez started to weed at one end. Baz and Alec at the other.

The soil was very stony and the sun was very hot. They soon took their shirts off, and still the sweat streamed down them. On and on, foot by foot, they picked and pulled and shuffled. At last, two hot hours after they had begun, they met in the middle.

'Stamp me!' said Baz, 'I'll stick to cattle in future!'

'My poor back,' groaned Tim.

They sat down on the bench outside the hut and the Hermit came out to pour very black coffee without milk into their hip flasks. Then they sat in silence while he glowered at them, making sure they drank every last, bitter drop.

Sanchez hated gaps in talking.

'You've got a nice place here,' he said. 'It grows some good weeds! Have you been here long?'

Very surprisingly the Hermit threw back his head and laughed. 'Ever since Broken World broke up,' he said.

'But that's nearly a hundred years ago!' said Alec. 'At the time of the Great War.'

'And I'm well over a hundred years old,' said the Hermit, looking a lot more pleased with himself. 'Hard work, wholesome food and plenty of your own company keep a man hale and hearty. I don't like company,' he added, looking cross again.

'Do you remember the Great War?' asked Alec. 'Where were you when the outsiders came with the fusion bombs and blew our planet up?'

'What outsiders?' asked the Hermit sharply.

'Why, the outsiders that wrecked everything

with their bombs when we were living peacefully on our little old planet,' replied Alec.

'Never were any outsiders,' said the Hermit shortly. 'It was just another cattle war. Someone wanted some pasture that someone else had got. One lot of blamed fool cattle men got hold of some fusion bombs they couldn't handle. Blew the whole place sky-high! No air! Bad time that was.'

He shook his old head, peering at them. 'I don't like cattle men. They never change.'

There was a complete silence outside the stone hut. Sanchez felt very sorry for Baz and Alec. So it had been the old struggle for land and cattle that had smashed their world to pieces. And the struggle was still going on now between the Maxwells and the Kenchs.

Baz would not look at anyone. He just stared at the dust.

'Say this though,' said the Hermit after a while, 'your Uncle Richard had some sense. But he got out of here. "Let 'em blow 'emselves up again," he said to me. "I'm off to Paris to enjoy myself." I reckon he knew what he was doing. Cattle and cattle men!' The Hermit spat in the dust.

'Still I promised him,' he continued, 'and here's what you're after.' He pulled a roll of brown papers fastened with sealing wax from his belt. 'Here's the title deeds to the Dorado Grand, much good may they do you!'

He thrust them into Baz's hand. Baz did not look at them.

'Fifteen thousand head of cattle on the Dorado Grand,' said the Hermit. 'How many head of cattle have you got already on your ranch?'

'Thirty thousand head,' said Baz dully.

'Heh!' laughed the Hermit, 'nice to be some folks! Well, I've got to get some sleep, so I'll say goodbye to you. Thanks for the bit of weeding.' He scowled at Sanchez and went into the hut. The door slammed.

Sadly they walked back to their punch-riders and, hardly saying a word, they rode back up to *Dragonfall 5* and knocked on the cabin door.

Big Mother and Old Elias listened carefully to every word of what had happened.

'And there it is!' said Baz gloomily pointing to the roll of brown papers. 'We got the Dorado Grand at last. But there don't seem much point in it.'

'I think,' said Big Mother slowly, 'we'd better pay a call on the Maxwells.'

Baz looked at her, then nodded. 'Happen we'd better,' he said.

Big Mother insisted on coming with them.

She was very nervous because she weighed more than fifteen stone, but Baz was splendid and said that she would go easily on the dog saddle of his punch-rider.

'Do you reckon it'll hold me?' she asked, standing on *Dragonfall*'s gangway.

'Ma'am,' replied Baz gallantly, 'you won't make no more difference than if you was a feather!'

All the same, it did a great dip when Big Mother sat down and it was all Baz could do to balance the magnetic forces.

Waving goodbye to Old Elias, who 'didn't hold with visiting', they rode very slowly across space to the brown ranch huts of the Maxwells. No one saw them as they sank down, guided by Sanchez, to the verandah of the Glory Hole. This was surrounded by a great cloud of dust and inside they could hear a tremendous grumbling.

'Ma! do we have to go on hunting? I don't believe the title deeds are here!'

'Ma! I've cut my hand on a rusty nail!'

'Ma! we've looked through this lot twice already!'

'Then look through it again, you idle no-goods! It's got to be somewhere.'

Inside, Lee, Danull, Dave Anderson and

Ma Maxwell, all looking very grubby and bad-tempered, were going on hands and knees through the mountain of junk where Sanchez had been imprisoned.

Ma Maxwell looked up as they got to the doorway.

'And what,' she roared, 'can we do for you?'

'I understand,' said Big Mother very politely, 'that my boys have played some sort of trick on your boys. So I've brought them along with me to straighten things out. Go on, Baz.'

'Well,' said Baz nervously, 'we've come to tell you that the voice you heard on the recording cylinder weren't Uncle Richard's at all! It was Sanchez here, sounding like Uncle Richard.'

'I knew it!' snapped Dave.

'Hold your tongue, Cousin Dave,' boomed Ma Maxwell.

'And the real place where the deeds to the Dorado Grand were hidden was on Hollow Hill, with the Hermit.'

'That old cattle thief!' said Danull.

'So you've got the deeds after all?' said Lee grimly.

'We've got them,' said Baz, looking red and awkward, 'but we don't want them.'

'What!' said Ma Maxwell.

'You see,' Baz continued, 'we got talking to

the old Hermit and he told us that the reason
Broken World got broken wasn't through any
outsiders in the Great War, like we thought.
It was us cattle folk that broke it ourselves
by chuckin' fusion bombs at each other.'

No one said anything, but Ma Maxwell

looked at Baz with an odd sad expression and nodded her head.

'So I got to thinking,' said Baz, smiling a little, 'that we got plenty of cattle and you got plenty of cattle, and there ain't neither of us really needs the Dorado Grand after all!

But I've brought the deeds to give to you in case you really need them.'

Baz put the roll of brown title deeds down on an old cattle skin in front of Lee. Lee looked at Ma Maxwell but she gave no sign.

'Reckon we don't need them either,' said Lee. He grinned, picked them up and handed them back. 'What are we going to do with them?'

'Well,' said Baz, 'the Condavees don't need the Dorado Grand because they don't eat meat. So how about sharing it out to the hired hands?'

And so it was settled. They all shook hands.

'But I feel sort of bad about the Condavees,' said Danull. 'I mean old Beel Dal Az was pretty good to us and we cheated him rotten. How about us all going over there to tell him what's happened?'

'Fine!' said Ma Maxwell, 'and Cousin Dave will stop here and help me put this Glory Hole back in shape. Reckon it's all he's good for!'

'Why!' said Big Mother, 'as to that, I think I'll stop here too and lend a hand. There's not much room for me on those dog saddles.'

'Now,' said Ma Maxwell with a beaming smile, 'I call that real neighbourly!'